A Gift

GIFT OF

THE JOHN & PEGGY

MAXIMUS

FUND

Published in the United States of America by The Child's World®
1980 Lookout Drive • Mankato, MN 56003-1705
800-599-READ • www.childsworld.com

ACKNOWLEDGMENTS
The Child's World®: Mary Berendes, Publishing Director
The Design Lab: Kathleen Petelinsek, Design and Page Production
Literacy Consultants: Cecilia Minden, PhD, and Joanne Meier, PhD

LIBRARY OF CONGRESS
CATALOGING-IN-PUBLICATION DATA
Moncure, Jane Belk.
  My "j" sound box / by Jane Belk Moncure ;
illustrated by Rebecca Thornburgh.
    p. cm. — (Sound box books)
  Summary: "Little j has an adventure with items beginning with
his letter's sound, such as jackrabbits, a jack-o'-lantern, and a
jaguar in the jungle."—Provided by publisher.
  ISBN 978-1-60253-150-5 (library bound : alk. paper)
  [1. Alphabet.] I. Thornburgh, Rebecca McKillip, ill. II. Title. III.
Series.
  PZ7.M739Myj 2009
  [E]–dc22   2008033166

Copyright ©2009 by The Child's World®
All rights reserved. No part of the book may be reproduced or
utilized in any form or by any means without written permission
from the publisher.

A NOTE TO PARENTS AND EDUCATORS:

Magic moon machines and five fat frogs are just a few of the fun things you can share with children by reading books with them. Reading aloud helps children in so many ways! It introduces them to new words, motivates them to develop their own reading skills, and expands their attention span and listening abilities. So it's important to find time each day to share a book or two . . . or three!

As you read with young children, you can help develop their understanding of how print works by talking about the parts of the book—the cover, the title, the illustrations, and the words that tell the story. As you read, use your finger to point to each word, modeling a gentle sweep from left to right.

Simple word games help develop important prereading skills, including an understanding of rhyme and alliteration (when words share the same beginning sound, such as "six" and "sand"). Try playing with words from a book you've just shared: "What other words start with the same sound as moon?" "Cat and hat, do those words rhyme?" The possibilities are endless—and so are the rewards!

My "j" Sound Box®

WRITTEN BY JANE BELK MONCURE

ILLUSTRATED BY REBECCA THORNBURGH

Little  had a box. "I will find

things that begin with my **j**

sound," he said. "I will put them

into my sound box."

But first, Little  put on his

jeans and jacket. "I will jump,"

he said.

He jumped over the box like a

jumping jack.

Then he jumped into the box.

"I am a  jack-in-the-box!" he

said. He jumped up.

Little  jumped up a hill.

"I will jump like Jack and Jill," he said. He jumped down the hill.

Then he saw a jack-o'-lantern.

Did he put the jack-o'-lantern

into his box? He did.

Then Little  jumped until he
saw jackrabbits.

The jackrabbits were jumping

everywhere!

Did he put the jumping jackrabbits

into the box with the jack-o'-lantern?

He did.

Then he jumped until he saw jays.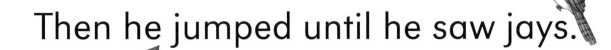

The jays cried, "Jay! Jay! Jay!"

Little  put them into the

box with the jack-o'-lantern

and the jackrabbits.

Now the box was full, so Little  found a jeep.

He put the box with the jackrabbits, jays, and jack-o'-lantern into the jeep and drove into the jungle.

Just then, Little  saw a jaguar.

The jaguar was about to jump

on the jackrabbits!

20

Little 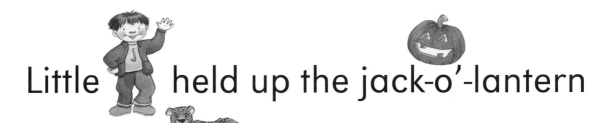 held up the jack-o'-lantern

and the jaguar jumped away!

Little 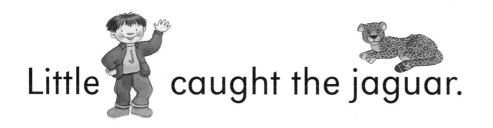 caught the jaguar.

He took her to jail so she could

not jump on the jackrabbits.

Just then, Little  saw Jumbo,

the jolly elephant.

"Jumbo is too big for my sound  box," he said.

Little  found a jet. A jumbo jet!

It was big enough for the animals

and everything else.

Little 's Word List

jacket

jack-in-the-box

jack-o'-lantern

jackrabbit

jaguar

jail

jay

jeans

jeep

jet

jungle

Other Words with Little

jackal		jelly		judge	
jacks		jellyfish		juggler	
jade		jewels		juice	
January		jigsaw puzzle		July	
jar		jockey		June	

More to Do!

Little  did lots of jumping in this book! He probably likes to jump rope, too. Do you like to jump rope? Here are some fun rhyming songs you can sing the next time you jump rope.

Rhyming Songs for Jumping Rope

Jack Be Nimble

Jack be nimble,
Jack be quick,
Jack jump over the candlestick.

Teddy Bear, Teddy Bear

Teddy bear, teddy bear, turn around.
Teddy bear, teddy bear, touch the ground.
Teddy bear, teddy bear, show your shoe.
Teddy bear, teddy bear, that will do!

Pease Porridge Hot

Pease porridge hot,
Pease porridge cold,
Pease porridge in the pot,
Nine days old.

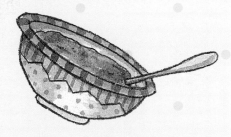

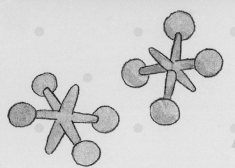

About the Author

Best-selling author Jane Belk Moncure has written over 300 books throughout her teaching and writing career. After earning a Master's degree in Early Childhood Education from Columbia University, she became one of the pioneers in that field. In 1956, she helped form the Virginia Association for Early Childhood Education, which established the first statewide standards for teachers of young children.

Inspired by her work in the classroom, Mrs. Moncure's books have become standards in primary education, and her name is recognized across the country. Her success is reflected not only in her books' popularity with parents, children, and educators, but also by numerous awards, including the 1984 C. S. Lewis Gold Medal Award.

About the Illustrator

Rebecca Thornburgh lives in a pleasantly spooky old house in Philadelphia. If she's not at her drawing table, she's reading—or singing with her band, called Reckless Amateurs. Rebecca has one husband, two daughters, and two silly dogs.